Puss in Boots

"YOUR MAJESTY, I HAVE BROUGHT YOU A LITTLE
PRESENT FROM MY MASTER"

(See p. 22)

PUSS IN BOOTS

RETOLD BY

E. E. ELLSWORTH

BLACKIE & SON LIMITED
LONDON AND GLASGOW

BLACKIE & SON LIMITED
5 Fitzhardinge Street
London, W.1
Bishopbriggs, Glasgow

BLACKIE & SON (INDIA) LIMITED
103/5 Fort Street, Bombay

Printed in Great Britain by Blackie & Son, Ltd., Glasgow

PUSS IN BOOTS

CHAPTER I

The Talking Cat

Once upon a time there was a miller. He had three sons. He loved them all very much indeed. But he loved the youngest son best.

When the miller died he left the eldest son the mill. The second had the donkey. The youngest son had nothing but the miller's cat.

The eldest son said:

" There is no room for you at the mill. There is barely enough for me. So you must go away, John."

John got ready to leave the mill. He felt very sad.

He put on his hat and coat. He tied all he had in a little bundle. He put it over his shoulder and away he went. He had not gone far when he saw

the cat was behind him.
"Oh, Puss!" he cried.
"Go back to the mill. I
have no food for you. I
have nothing for myself.
But there are rats and
mice at the mill. Run

along there, Puss. You will starve if you come with me."

But the cat said:

"Oh no, master. Do take me with you. I will make your fortune."

The miller's son was so astonished, he could hardly speak. He stared at the cat.

"Can you talk?" he cried. "How wonderful! I never knew cats could speak."

"Have you any money?"

the clever cat asked next.

"Only one piece," replied the miller's son.

"Then please buy me a pair of boots. That is the one thing I want to make me happy."

"I will buy you some boots," said the delighted John.

Together they went to the nearest town. There they bought a splendid pair of boots for the cat. He was full of joy.

"Now I am Puss in

Boots. Please call me Puss, master."

"Very well, Puss," said John. "Is there anything else I can buy for you?"

"Yes, master. I want a strong bag with a string at the top," said the cat. "It is not for myself. It will be for you."

"But I do not want a bag," said the miller's son.

"Never mind that," said Puss. "Please buy one and then give it to me."

The young man bought

a good strong bag. It had
string threaded through
the top to open and shut it.
Puss seemed very pleased
indeed. He pranced along
the road in great glee.

By and by they came

to some fine woods and broad open fields. There was a little hut just at the edge of the woods.

" This is our new home," said Puss. " We shall live very happily here, master."

" I do not think much of this place," said the miller's son. " It is not like the nice clean mill."

" Never mind," said Puss. " You shall soon have a much better one. You shall have one fit for a king."

But the miller's son only laughed, and said:

"Oh no, Puss. I am afraid that is not likely to happen. Remember, after all, I am only the son of a miller."

"To me you are a Prince," said the faithful Puss, "and my dear master."

That night, as there was no bed, they slept on the floor of the hut.

Early the next morning Puss got up. He took the

bag and some lettuce. Then he went away to the forest. There were hundreds of rabbits in the forest.

Puss put the bag in front of a rabbit hole. He put the lettuce inside the bag. Then he opened the bag as wide as he could. Close by were some thick bushes. Puss hid himself in the bushes and waited.

By and by out popped two fine young rabbits.

They smelt the lettuce in the bag. Then they hopped inside to nibble it.

That was just what Puss wanted. He had been holding the string in his paws. He pulled it tight and caught them. Then away he went along the road.

Soon he came to the king's castle. He knocked at the door.

"I want to see the king," he said to the servants.

They were astonished to see a cat with boots on. They were still more astonished to hear him talk. So they brought him to the king. Puss bowed very low to the king.

"Good morning, your majesty," he said. " I have brought a present from my master."

He laid the rabbits at the king's feet.

" Who is your master?" asked the surprised king.

"My master is the Marquis of Carabas," replied the cat.

"Please thank your master for his kind present," said the king. "They are very fine rabbits."

He gave the cat a piece of gold money. Puss thanked him and hurried back to John.

"Look, master!" he cried. "Here is some money for you. Take it and buy something to eat."

The miller's son was feeling very hungry. So he took the money. Then off he went to get some food for himself and for the clever puss.

CHAPTER II

The Marquis of Carabas

A few days afterwards Puss got up very early. He took the bag. But he did not put any lettuces inside. He put some wheat instead. Then off he went. He had seen some fine partridges the day before.

He opened the bag as wide as he could. Inside

were the grains of wheat.

By and by some par-
tridges came along. The
partridges began to peck
at the wheat. They liked
the taste. So they went
right inside the bag.

"Aha!" thought Puss.
"Now I have got you."
He pulled the strings of
the bag. The birds were
caught.

So Puss went once
more to the king. He
bowed very low.

"Good morning, your

majesty," he said. "I have brought you a little present from my master."

"How very kind of the Marquis of Carabas," said the king. "They are very fine partridges. Where did they come from?"

"From the woods of the Marquis of Carabas," replied clever Puss.

"Please thank your master very much," said the king. "I should like to see him. Please tell him to call at the castle."

Now the king had a very beautiful daughter. Puss had seen her. He said she was the most beautiful princess in the world.

"Master," he said one day. "I think you ought to marry the princess." The miller's son laughed.

"Oh, poor Puss," he said. "You must be mad to think such a thing."

But the cat said:

"We shall see. Strange things often happen."

After that Puss very often went to the king. Sometimes he took rabbits. Sometimes he took partridges. Sometimes he took a fine hare.

Each time he said to the king: "A little present from my master, the Marquis of Carabas."

Soon the king began to think about the Marquis of Carabas.

"I should like to see this young Marquis," he said. "He is very kind to send me such nice presents. He must be a rich young man."

The princess said:

"Yes, Father, he seems to be a very nice Marquis."

"We will go for a drive by the river," said the king. "Perhaps we shall meet the Marquis of Carabas."

Directly Puss heard this he ran home.

"Master," he said. "I want you to go and bathe

in the cool, clear river."

"But I do not want to bathe in the river," said John. "I would rather stay as I am."

"Oh, please do," cried the cat. "Please go and bathe in the river. Do, do, master."

Now the miller's son was a kind young man. He did not like to upset the cat. So he said:

"Oh, very well then, Puss. I will go and bathe in the river."

"Thank you, master," said Puss. "You will not be sorry afterwards. But be as quick as you can."

John ran down to the river. He undressed quickly and jumped in. He began to swim about.

When he was not looking, Puss took his clothes. He hid them under a big stone. Then he ran out to the road. He looked along it. He saw the king's carriage. Then he began to shout:

"Help, help! The Marquis of Carabas is drowning!"

The king heard him. He stopped the carriage and said: "What is the matter?"

"Oh, your majesty,"

cried Puss. "My master, the Marquis of Carabas, is drowning."

"Dear, dear," said the king. "We must not let the poor Marquis drown." He called two of his servants. "Go and help the Marquis," he said.

The two servants soon helped John out of the water. But they could not find his clothes. Puss pretended to look for them. But he did not find them. So the king said to one of his servants at once:

" Run as fast as you can and bring a nice suit of clothes for the Marquis."

Soon the servant came back with some fine clothes. The miller's son put them on. He looked very handsome indeed.

Then he went to speak to the king. The king thought to himself: "What a handsome young man!"

So he said:

"Would you like to come for a drive, my lord Marquis?"

"I should like it very much," said John.

Now Puss could run very fast. He ran along the road in front of the carriage. Soon he came to some lovely fields. There were some men in them. They were making hay. Puss went up to them.

"The king is coming this way," he said. "He is in his carriage with the princess. Very likely he will stop. He will ask about these hay fields. You must say that they belong to the Marquis of Carabas. If you do not, you will be chopped into mincemeat."

The haymakers promised to do as Puss told

them. They did not want
to be chopped into mince-
meat.

Then Puss ran on again.
Soon he came to some
large fields. They were
full of corn. Some men
were in the fields. Puss
ran up to them and said:
"The king is coming
this way. He is in his
carriage with the princess.
He will ask you about these
corn fields. You must say
that they belong to the
Marquis of Carabas. If

you do not, you will be chopped into mincemeat."

The men were very much afraid. They promised to do what Puss told them. They did not want to be chopped into mincemeat.

Puss ran on. This time he came to some lovely green fields. All over the fields were sheep. They were very nice sheep. Some of them had lambs with them. There were shepherds in the fields, too. They were minding the sheep.

Puss in Boots marched up to them.

"The king is coming this way," he said. "He is driving in his carriage

with the princess. He will stop, to see these lovely sheep. Then he will say: 'Whose sheep are these?' You must say: 'They belong to the Marquis of Carabas.' If you do not, you will be chopped into mincemeat."

Now the shepherds were afraid, too, of Puss. So they said: "We will do just as you tell us."

Puss in Boots felt very pleased with himself.

On he ran once more.

CHAPTER III

The Marquis's Lands

Soon the king came along in his carriage. He looked out of the window. He saw the hay fields.

"Stop," he said to his servants. "I want to look at these lovely hay fields."

Then he spoke to the men.

"To whom do these hay fields belong?"

"They belong to the

Marquis of Carabas," replied the men.

"You have some very fine fields of hay," said the king. "Why, they are better than mine, my dear Marquis."

"They are indeed fine hay fields," replied the miller's son.

"Drive on," said the king.

So the servants drove on again.

By and by they came to the fields of corn.

"Stop!" cried the king. "I must look at these corn fields. They are the best I have ever seen. Come here," he said to the men in the fields. "Whose corn fields are these?"

"They belong to the Marquis of Carabas," replied the men. They did not want to be chopped into mincemeat.

The king was delighted with the corn fields.

On went the carriage once more. Soon they

came to the shepherds. They were with the sheep and lambs. The king looked at the flocks.

"Whose sheep are these?" he said to the shepherds.

"They belong to the Marquis of Carabas," replied the shepherds.

"Indeed," said the king. "They are very fine animals. I have never seen better ones."

CHAPTER IV

The Ogre's Castle

Soon Puss came to a very fine castle. It was as large as the king's castle. It was just as good, too.

In this castle there lived a big ogre. He was a very horrid ogre. Nobody liked him. His servants were afraid of him.

Puss came up to the

door.   He rang the big
bell.

"I want to see your
master," he said to the
servants.

"Our master is an ogre,"
said   one   servant.   He

thought Puss would run away. But Puss was not scared at all.

"Take me to see your master," he said.

So the servants took him to the ogre. The ogre was not polite like the king. He spoke in a loud cross voice.

"Who are you?" he said loudly.

"I am Puss in Boots," replied Puss boldly.

"What do you want here?" asked the ogre.

His voice was still very gruff.

"I have come to see you, Sir Ogre," said Puss in Boots. "I hear that you are so wonderful."

This made the ogre very pleased. He puffed himself up with pride.

"You are right," he said. "I am very clever and very wonderful as well. Sit down and we will talk together."

So Puss sat down on a chair. He looked at the

ogre and said loudly:

"You are very big, Sir Ogre."

"Yes," said the ogre. "I am a fine big ogre."

"I hear that you can change yourself into something else," said Puss. "But I can hardly believe it."

"It is quite true," said the ogre. "I can change into anything I like."

"Can you change yourself into a lion?" asked Puss.

"Yes," replied the ogre. "Watch me and you will see."

In a twinkling he changed himself into a lion. He roared up and down the room. He looked so fierce that Puss was afraid of him. He sprang up on the window-sill. Then the ogre changed himself to his right shape.

"Ho! ho! ho!" he laughed. "You can come down now. Don't you think I am clever?"

"Yes, indeed," said Puss. "I was quite scared, Sir Ogre. You made such a fierce lion."

"I can do anything I like," boasted the ogre. "I can change myself into an elephant, or a whale too."

"Well!" said Puss. "I have seen you as something very large. Now could you change into something small?"

"Of course," said the ogre. "Shall I change into a dog?"

"Something smaller than that, please, Sir Ogre," said Puss.

"A rat, then?" asked the ogre.

"Could you change into a little mouse?" said

that clever Puss in Boots.

"Certainly," said the ogre. He changed himself into a tiny mouse. He ran across the floor.

Quick as a flash Puss sprang at him. He caught the mouse in his paws and

killed him. Then he ate him.

"Aha, Sir Ogre!" he said. "That is the end of you."

He felt very pleased with himself. Then he went to find the servants.

"You will never see the ogre again," he said. "He has gone for good. The castle now belongs to the Marquis of Carabas. You are all his servants.

"Now you must prepare a fine dinner. He will

soon be here. The king is coming, too. So is the princess."

The castle was not very clean. So the servants brought some pails of hot water and soap. They scrubbed the floors and made them clean. They spread rich carpets down everywhere. They brought out big dishes of gold and silver. They unlocked the ogre's cupboards and found silver and gold cups and mugs. They found knives, forks, and spoons of silver and gold, too.

Then they cooked chicken, ducks, geese, and pigs for dinner.

Then Puss ran out into the gardens.

"Hurry up," he cried to the gardeners. "Your new master will want these gardens to look nice." The gardeners did as Puss told them.

Then Puss ran to the stables.

"Your new master is

the Marquis of Carabas," he said. "The ogre is dead. You need not fear him any more. Now you must look after the horses. You must brush them well. You must make their coats shine like satin. Then you must clean the carriage, too."

The men in the stables were glad that the ogre was dead.

"We will work hard for our new master," they said.

Then Puss ran down to the castle gate. He looked down the road. The king's carriage was coming along. Soon it reached the gates.

"Stop!" said the king.

"I want to look at this fine castle. I have never seen it before. Whose castle is this?"

"It belongs to the Marquis of Carabas," said Puss in Boots.

"My dear Marquis," said the king. "What a fine castle you have. I am delighted with it."

"Will you come in, your majesty?" asked Puss in Boots. "You must be hungry after your long drive. Dinner will be ready in a few moments."

"Would you like to come in, my dear?" said the king. He turned to the princess.

"Yes," she replied. "I should like to see inside this lovely castle."

"Very well, then," said the king. "We will come in. I am feeling rather hungry myself."

As they got out of the carriage, John said:

"Whose castle is this, Puss?" He spoke in a

whisper. He did not want the king to hear.

"Do not be afraid," said Puss. "The ogre is dead. I have eaten him. So now the castle is yours."

They all went into the castle. The miller's son looked very handsome as he walked in, and the cat said: "Make way for the king and the princess. Make way for the Marquis of Carabas, your master."

Inside the castle was all ready. Everything was

spick and span. They
came into the dining-
room and sat down to din-
ner. How surprised the
king was to see such a
lovely dinner. He was
more surprised to see all
the gold and silver.

"My dear Marquis," he said. "You must be very rich. You have a splendid castle. And this is a splendid dinner."

"My master is very rich indeed," said Puss proudly. "He has some fine cellars. In the cellars are sacks and sacks of gold. My master is the richest man in these parts."

"Indeed," said the king in great surprise.

So they were all very merry. The miller's son

kept looking at the princess. He thought she was the loveliest princess in the world. She thought he was the handsomest man in the world. Then the king thought:

"I like this young man. I think he would make a nice son-in-law. He is very good-looking. He is very rich, too. I am sure he likes the princess, and she likes him. I will see what she says about it."

So after dinner he said

quietly to his daughter:

"My dear, do you like this Marquis?"

"Yes, Father," she replied. "I like him very much indeed. I think he would make a good, kind husband."

"So do I," said the king. "I will speak to him about it."

Later on the king said:

"How do you like the princess, my lord Marquis?"

"Oh, I think she is beautiful," replied John. "I have never seen anybody like her."

"Well, then," said the king, "how would you like to marry her, my boy?"

"Oh, indeed, sir," said John, "I am not nearly

good enough to marry her."

"Well, I think you are," said the king. "So we will see about the wedding."

He smiled at John and looked very happy. The princess looked very happy, too. But John was not happy.

So he told the king the truth. Then he felt much happier. He told the king all about his clever cat.

The king said:

"If your clever Puss

has killed the ogre, the castle is yours. He has earned it for you. So you can still be the Marquis of Carabas. You can marry the princess."

So John became the real Marquis of Carabas. He married the princess and they were very happy indeed. He was always kind to his dear Puss. And Puss stayed with him as long as he lived. He became the very famous Puss in Boots.

MORE ABOUT
BRENDA BEAR

MORE ABOUT
BRENDA BEAR

MARION COOMBES

Illustrated by Jenny Reyn

BLACKIE: LONDON & GLASGOW

Blackie & Son Ltd., 5 Fitzhardinge Street, London, W.1
17 Stanhope Street, Glasgow
Blackie & Son (India) Ltd., Bombay; Blackie & Son (Canada) Ltd., Toronto

Printed in Great Britain by Blackie & Son, Ltd., Glasgow

CONTENTS

BRENDA BEAR WAS MAKING A PUDDING

I

THE FLOWER SHOW

Brenda Bear was making a pudding when Duckling rushed in, very excited.

"A little bird told me," he gasped, "that there is going to be another book about *us*!"

"Which little bird?"

asked Brenda. "There are so many little birds, and they tell you such funny things."

"This was my very special little bird," said Duckling. "He only tells me the most important *true* things. He said there will be another book about you, Brenda dear, and Sir Puffer Train, and Froggy, and me! Isn't it wonderful? I wonder what we shall be doing in the new book. I wonder if there will be a picture of me in my new coat?"

Brenda Bear laughed her cuddly laugh. " It will be wonderful," she agreed, " but I'm sure we shan't be doing anything special in the new book. We shall just be spending days and nights as we always do; the children who read the book will peep inside it to see what we are doing; perhaps they will see a picture of the flowers we have been growing for the Flower Show."

Froggy arrived just as
Brenda spoke. "When the
children look into the new
book about us, they will be
surprised to see no
flowers at all in Duck-
ling's garden," he said.
"They will only see
weeds! Duckling didn't
bother to grow any
flowers, did you, Duck-
ling?"

Duckling looked sad. " I
meant to, but I kind of
forgot," he said. " I'll go

and grow some quickly now."

Froggy laughed loudly, but Brenda said, "Oh Duckling, you can't grow flowers in time for the Show tomorrow; nobody can make flowers hurry up and grow. Perhaps there will be some other kind of prize that you can win."

Poor Duckling tried hard not to cry, but he sat out on the step looking very unhappy, and when Sir Puffer Train saw him, he felt unhappy too.

Suddenly Sir Puff smiled. "I know! Come with me," he said. "I will help you win a prize, but it will be hard work for you. Will you try?"

"Oh yes," cried Duckling happily, "I'll try my very hardest. What will I have to do?"

Puff whispered something—and whatever that something was, it made Duckling climb up and drive away on good, kind Puff, away to the fields

and woods, and neither of
them were seen again for
a long, long time.

Brenda Bear wore her best hat at the Flower Show. When she won the first prize for her roses, she went pink all over, right down to her toes. When the flowers had all been judged, the Mayor said that the wild flowers, arranged in vases and bowls, would be judged next.

There were lots of pretty little jars and posies, but in the middle there was a huge bowl with more wild flowers in it than Brenda had ever seen. Everybody called out that it should have the prize, but the Mayor said "Hush, everybody! There is something more to do before the prize is won. All the wild flowers in the bowl must be *named*! Come forward, the owner of this wonderful collection. If you know the names of all your flowers, the prize will be yours."

To Brenda Bear's astonishment, Duckling went forward, very smart in his new coat.

"Oh dear," thought Brenda, "he will not know their names! He can't even remember his two times table." And she felt sad for Duckling.

But listen—what was
his? Beginning with
Buttercup, Daisy, and all
he easy ones, Duckling
went on, and on, and on.
He named Rock-rose and
Speedwell, Self-heal and
Ground-ivy, Dogs Mercury
and Wood Spurge . . . on
and on and on, until the
Mayor cried "Stop! You
have won the prize. I
didn't think one small
duckling could possibly
remember so many
flowers."

Then Duckling went pink all over, just as Brenda had, and he took his prize.

Do you remember that little bird who told Duckling true things? Well, he was at the Flower Show, too, and he whispered something to the Mayor. After listening the Mayor replied "That is most interesting. Thank you for telling me, Little Bird." Then he said "Ladies and gentleman. There is one more prize, a very special one. It is a prize for the Kindest Heart, and it goes to Sir Puffer Train, for teaching Duckling how to find, and name, all these flowers."

This was such a lovely surprise that everybody went pink with joy. Then they went home, saying what a good idea it was to have a Flower Show.

II
REAL HIDE AND SEEK

Nobody had seen Froggy for a long time and, when tea-time came, there was still no sign of him. Brenda Bear was quite worried; there were so many places a frog might be, that you did not know where to begin to look.

Duckling was no help at all; he just sat in a pool of tears which he had made by crying ever since Frog was missing.

At first he hadn't cared; he and Frog had been playing hide and seek, and so when he couldn't find Froggy at all, he had thought, "Oh well, he has won this game, because I can't find him anywhere." And then Duckling had gone shopping for Brenda.

But when lunch-time came, where was that hungry Frog? He was nowhere. They looked everywhere. They looked under the stairs, where it is too dark even to dust, and Duckling got covered with cobwebs. Then they got the step-ladder and looked on the top shelf in the kitchen, and in the broom-cupboard, and in the pantry, and under the wood-pile. But everywhere they looked, there was just no Froggy at all —and now it was tea-time.

Suddenly Sir Puffer puffed in. He had been out all day so he didn't

know that Froggy was
missing.

"Don't worry," Sir Puffer said. "We'll soon find him. Stop crying, Duckling, dear. Crying never found anybody. And don't worry, Brenda, because I feel in my wheels that we shall find Froggy before bedtime."

Then Sir Puff asked Duckling to tell him some of the places they had hidden in on other days when they played hide and seek.

Duckling thought hard. "In the ironing basket,"

he said, "or just a little
way up the chimney, or in
the little cupboard on the
landing; sometimes we
hide in easy places like
behind the curtains, or a
door. Once Froggy hid in
the pocket of Brenda's
going - to - get - the - coal - in
coat—"

"Oh, *no!*" cried Brenda.
"Oh dear and good
gracious *no!*"

"Now don't get ex-
cited," said Puff. "A coat
pocket is quite a cosy

place to hide in. Much better than up the chimney."

"Yes, but I don't *give the chimney away!*" wailed Brenda. "I gave that old coat to the Jumble Sale, just before lunch. Quickly, Puff dear, take us there at once. Perhaps they won't have sold it yet."

In a few minutes they were on their way. As soon as they reached the Village Hall, Brenda and

Duckling rushed in and
found the coat stall.

"Please," gasped Bren-
da, "have you a very old
coat with coal dust on it?"

"I'm afraid not, mad-
am," said the lady who

was minding the stall, "but we have a nice fur coat, if you would like that."

"Oh dear, no thank you," said Brenda. "I have a fur coat all over me —it is part of me, you know. What I want is a very old getting-the-coal-in coat which I gave to the Jumble man this morning. I think there is something of ours in the pocket of it."

"I remember that

coat!" cried the lady. "It had a very nice coaly smell. It was sold the moment we got it, to a chimney sweep who said the coal marks wouldn't matter at all, as he is always black."

When Brenda asked where the sweep lived, she was told it was far, far away, over the other side of the mountain, but you can guess Puff started off straight away, puffing and blowing round and

round the narrow mount-
ain paths. Duckling said it

made him feel funny look-
ing down the steep mount-
ain side, but Brenda said
"Then don't look!" be-
cause she really couldn't
be bothered about Duck-
ling when he was safe
beside her, and poor
Froggy lost and belonging
to a chimney sweep who
might not understand him
at all.

At last, after a frighten-
ing journey, they found
the sweep's house.

"That old coat?" he

said. "Why, it's out in the shed. I hope you don't want it back. I paid sixpence for it."

"Oh no," said Brenda. "We only want our Froggy back, out of the pocket."

"You are welcome to *him*," said the sweep. "Frogs in my pocket are things I don't care for at all." He unlocked the shed, and there, waiting to be rescued, was darling Froggy! They all hugged

him and drove home all
over the mountain again,
and were back before bed-
time, just as Puff had
said.

Before they went to sleep, Duckling and Froggy decided not to play hide and seek again for quite a while.

"I don't somehow like it as much as I did," said Froggy.

III

BRENDA BEAR'S HEDGE

The hedge round
Brenda Bear's little house
had grown so high that
the little house itself was
almost hidden from sight.

"Nobody will know
there is a house here,"
said Duckling sadly.
"Sometimes, when we

come from school, I don't remember there is a house here, and I wonder where I live."

"Silly one!" laughed Brenda. All the same, she knew that she must find someone to cut the hedge, before it began to keep the sunshine out of their rooms.

Puff was puzzled, because Brenda Bear could do most things herself.

"Why must we wait for somebody *else* to cut our

very own hedge?" Puff asked. "Why don't we do it ourselves?"

Brenda Bear explained. "Hedges are rather special," she said. "Hedges have to be quite straight, and very neat. They're much harder to cut than grass. No, we must wait until a special hedge-cutting man comes round."

So they waited.

Now, one day a man called and asked if Brenda

wanted any knives or
scissors sharpened.

"Well, yes," said
Brenda, "but I'd rather
you cut the hedge."

"I can't cut hedges,"
said the scissor-grinder,
"and certainly not a great

big hedge like that
Hedges are rather special
One day a hedge-cutting
man may come this way
so I'd better sharpen the
shears, too."

So he did, and he also
sharpened the nail
scissors, the dress-making
scissors, the garden
scissors for cutting flowers
with, and the kitchen
scissors for cutting everything with. "They are all
nice and sharp now, Ma-
dam," he said to Brenda

so she paid him and off he went.

Now Duckling had been very interested in all that sharpening, and he longed to have a little cut to see just how sharp the scissors were.

"No," said Froggy, "you know we mustn't touch scissors unless Brenda is here."

"And when she *is* here, she won't let us because she'll say they're too sharp!" said naughty

Duckling. "So I'm going to have a wee cut now." And he did.

There was something lovely about cutting with

really sharp scissors, and Duckling felt he must go on cutting, so he went into the garden and cut a teeny bit of hedge. It was so easy! Froggy had a wee cut too, because cutting is a very catching thing.

"If we stood on Puff we could cut the top of the hedge," said Duckling. "Then we could see the house again, and Brenda Bear would be pleased."

Puff agreed to let them climb up on him, but he

also gave his little private
"toot" which mean
"Brenda come quickly and
stop Duckling doing
something".

Quickly Brenda came
running, all ready to say
"Don't, Duckling." But
this time she didn't say it
Instead, she went and pu
on her jeans and her gar
den hat and brought out
the shears. Then she stood
on Puff, too, and began to
cut the hedge.

Everything would have

been all right if Brenda hadn't gone to see how the dinner was getting on. While she was indoors Duckling began to do a bit of funny cutting. "Look," he cried, "I've made a shape like *me*!"

Then Froggy started cutting very fast. "I'm going to make a shape like *me*, too," he said.

By the time Brenda Bear came back they had started cutting a shape like Puff, on the biggest piece

of hedge, and Brenda saw
that it was too late to stop
them, for, although you
can cut things *off*, you
can't cut them on again!

"You are both really naughty," said Brenda, but she didn't sound properly cross. "I'll help you finish Puff, then we'd better cut me into the hedge too."

So they did.

After that it was easy for everybody to find Brenda Bear's house, because the hedge had little models of them all, standing in a row.

IV

BEDTIME AT BRENDA'S

Every evening, when
Brenda Bear said "Time
for bed, dears", Duckling
and Froggy said they
weren't tired, and couldn't
they have a little longer.
Sometimes Duckling said
it, sometimes Frog said it,
and sometimes they *both*

said it together. This began to worry Brenda, because people who are late to bed don't want to get up in the morning, and that is a worry too.

"It makes me feel I am always grumbling at them," Brenda told Puff sadly. "Please will *you* tell them when it is bedtime tonight? You will have to be firm, and say it as if you mean it."

"Leave it to me," said

Sir Puff kindly. "Some-
times I think you are too
gentle with them. I shall
be very firm indeed, and
they'll be up in bed in no
time."

So Brenda began to
look forward to a nice
peaceful evening, and promised not to interfere at
all, but to leave it all to
Puff, who felt quite happy
about it.

After tea, Brenda played
games with Frog and
Duckling as usual, then

she went away to prepare
their supper, and turn on
the bath.

"Come on, time for bed" said Puff, in a no nonsense voice, "Put everything away."

But Frog and Duckling seemed suddenly to have become deaf, for they took no notice at all, but just went on building a castle with their bricks.

"I said time for bed!" repeated Puff in a louder voice.

"Do move back a bit, Puff dear," said Duckling. "You're in the way of the moat.   Pass that green brick, Froggy, please."

Those two went on playing, as if Puff had not spoken at all!

"For the last time . . ." Puff began in a very loud voice, but Froggy said "Do stop worrying us, Puff dear—you are spoiling our game.   Brenda will tell us when it's bedtime.   Besides, we're not tired.   We never are."

Sir Puff felt dreadful!

Soon Brenda Bear came

in with the supper tray. She was most surprised to see those two naughty ones still playing, and she had to laugh to herself when she saw poor Puff's red face.

"Never mind," she whispered to him. "I think I've had a good idea."

At last, when Frog and Duckling were really in bed, Brenda told Sir Puff what her idea was.

"How clever!" he cried. "I'll help you tomorrow morning, as soon as they've gone to school."

Next evening when Brenda said it was time for bed, it was Duckling who said "Oh, not yet. I'm not tired at all. I guess I'm one of those ducklings who don't need any sleep at all."

"Quite possibly," said Brenda Bear calmly. "Well, good night, dears. Puff and I are very tired, so we are going to bed."

Soon the house was quiet, except for Duckling and Frog playing.

"It's funny," said Duckling, after a little while, "but I don't feel like playing any more."

"Nor do I," said Froggy.

"I wish," said Duckling, "that somebody

would tell us to go to bed, don't you?"

"Yes," agreed Frog. "Let's go."

So up they went, forgetting all about supper and bathing, in their hurry to go to bed.

But oh, when they reached their room, what a shock they had! "Our beds have gone," they cried. "What a lot of floor and no beds!"

Now having no bed, when you are tired, is a

terrible thing. Duckling and Froggy sat down on all that great big empty floor and howled loudly. At once Brenda came in, wearing her dressing-gown.

"No beds?" she echoed. "But you two don't *need* beds! You are never tired! Every night you tell me you are not tired. I thought you would like to have this lovely big space to play in, and not have beds."

"We want to go to bed!" sobbed Duckling and Froggy. "Please, please let us go to bed, Brenda dear."

"Well, your beds are up in the loft," said Brenda, "and so, just for tonight, I'll make room for you in my bed, if you are quite sure you want to go to sleep. Come along."

As they curled up for the night, Sir Puff, who had been watching, closed his door softly.

"Brenda Bear is the most wonderful bear in the world," he said, but nobody heard him, because they were all asleep.

PATCH

PATCH CHASES THE SNOWBALLS

(See page 58)

PATCH

BY

E. E. ELLSWORTH

BLACKIE & SON LIMITED
LONDON AND GLASGOW

BLACKIE & SON LIMITED
5 Fitzhardinge Street
London, W.1
17 Stanhope Street, Glasgow

BLACKIE & SON (INDIA) LIMITED
103/5 Fort Street, Bombay

Printed in Great Britain by Blackie & Son, Ltd., Glasgow

PATCH

CHAPTER I

Patch leaves Fairbank Farm

My real name is Fairbank Dandy, but I have always been called "Patch" because of a large brown patch which I have over each eye.

It was Fred of Fairbank Farm who called me Patch. My mother belonged to him, and so of course did my

two brothers, my sister and
myself.

We were all born at the
farm, and thought it the
most wonderful place in the
world. There were so many
things to see, to bark at,
and sometimes to be scared
of too.

There were cows and
horses—so big that at first
I was afraid of them, and
thought they were giants.

There were chickens that
ran about the farm all day
long, big ones and little

nes.   The big ones looked
ierce.   They stretched their

ecks   and   made   such   a
unny   noise — my   mother
alled it crowing.

I am sorry to say I used to chase the tiny ones until my mother happened to see me one day, and gave me a severe scolding. I felt very ashamed of myself after it and promised never to do it again.

At the farm there was a big yard where my mother's kennel stood. Her name was Topsy and she was a fox terrier. We had glorious times playing round the kennel, and in the yard too. We got into mischief many times, I am afraid, but our mother was so kind and good that we were very soon sorry for our naughty ways.

"Remember, my dears," she used to say, "that you are the children of prize-winners! Our master has a beautiful silver cup which he told me I won for him. Besides, your father was a very handsome dog, and quite famous too. You must always remember that and try to be good little dogs."

We always listened very
carefully to our mother's

advice, and made up ou
minds to try to be as good
and clever as she was.

I well remember the day I left my home, and my dear mother. It was warm and sunny and I was tumbling about on the grass in front of the house with my brothers and sister. Fred our master came round the corner of the house with a very tall man.

I ran up to him and smelt him. Then as he was talking quietly to my master, I decided he was not an enemy and ran back to where my mother was lying.

I woke up my sister who
was beside her, by giving
a playful chew to her ear
She tried to bite my nose
and we were in the middle
of a glorious game when
our master called me.

had been taught to come
directly I was called, so
ran my fastest. In fact
ran so fast that I tumbled
over, but I jumped up and
stood in front of him, wag
ging my tail to show how
pleased I was.

He picked me up and the

tranger looked at me—at
ny teeth and felt me all
over.

"Yes," he said, "he cer-
ainly is a fine little puppy
and will make a good dog!"

He patted my head, and
I was so glad that I gave
him a friendly lick. I was
most excited when I heard
him say:

"I like this one best and
will take him to-day!"

He put me down and I
ran to my mother. I told
her what he had said, and

thought of course she would
be coming too. When she
said very proudly that she
had heard our master say
many times he would never
part with her, I did not feel
so happy about it. I cheered
up a little when she said I
should have a fine chance
to see the world and learn
many things. She made
me promise to be a good
little dog, to be obedient
and to be faithful and true
to my new master.

I was just telling my

brothers and sister all about it, and feeling very impor-

tant too, when Fred called me. So I said "Good-bye" to them all, and ran to him.

He picked me up and hugged me.

"Good-bye, old chap!" he said. "You're off to your new home to-day. I hope you grow up as good a dog as your mother."

Then the tall man took me, and we went through a field and on to the high-road. There was a large motor there with a lady sitting in it. I had seen motors, but I had never been in one before, and I was very frightened when

t began to move. It made
. strange noise, and as I did
10t like it I tried to jump out.
The lady put me on her
ap, however, and cuddled
ne, so that I was not afraid
any more, and went to sleep.

CHAPTER II

A New Master

I woke up just as the
motor stopped at a big gate.
A man opened it and we
got out. Then the lady
took me into a large house,

up some stairs, and into a
room. There was a little
boy lying on the sofa.

"Look, Peter," she said
"here is a little playmate
for you."

The little boy sat up and
took me in his arms. "Oh
Mummy!" he said. "Isn'
he jolly? I love him already
and he is my very own
isn't he?"

"Yes, Peter boy," said
the tall man, coming into
the room. "He is your
own, and is a jolly little

fellow. You'll be great
friends."

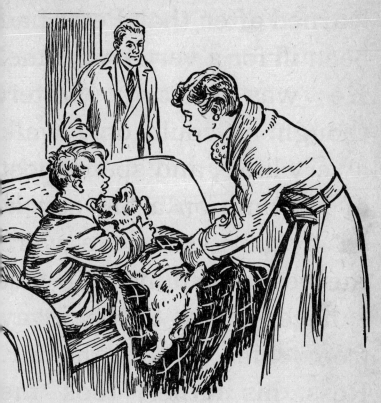

Then I knew that Peter
was to be my master, and I
made up my mind then and

there that I would love him
and obey him always.   I
learned after that Peter had
been ill for a very long time.
He was getting better,
though he could only walk
a very little, and spent most
of his time on a big couch.
In a short time we were
the best of chums.   In fact
I never liked to be away
from him, although Mr.
Ross, his father, took me
out for a walk every day,
and sometimes I played
about in the garden.

There were other people n the house besides Mr. and Mrs. Ross and Peter.

There was a person called James, who cleaned the motor, and sometimes drove t. Another one was called Mary. She used to set the tables, and bring in nice smelling dinners. Then there was one called Cook, who generally stayed in the kitchen. She did not like me very much, and got cross with me very often. Indeed, I heard her call me

"that tiresome dog", though
I really could not understand
why. I tried to be most

friendly to her, and often
jumped up and gave a little
tug at her sleeve, just to

how I would like to have
little game with her.
However, she did not seem
o like it as Peter did.

One day I came in from
he garden, where I had
ust buried a lovely bone. I
vas feeling very happy, so I
umped up to have a game
vith Cook. She screamed
ınd dropped a lot of hot
soup on the floor and on
ne too. I gave such a
yelp and ran under the
table. Even then she was
still cross with me, although

my poor back felt terribly
sore. But Mary was very
kind; she took me up to
Peter, who hugged me for
a long time. So I told him
as best I could how sorry
I was, and that I only
meant to be friendly.

Peter was a splendid
master and taught me many
tricks. I always listened
to him and tried to do
exactly as he told me. After
a while I learned them. I
could sit on my hind legs
and balance a lump o

sugar on my nose. And
I could toss it up in the

air and catch it when
Peter said: "It's yours,
Patch." I lay down quite

still when he said: "Die
for your country," and
also learned to march up
and down like a soldier.
When he said: "Halt!" I
stopped. Sometimes after
tea Peter would make me
do all my tricks to show
his father and mother.
When I had done them all
they always said I was a
clever little dog. That used
to please Peter very much
and he generally gave me
a piece of chocolate.

Once it was Peter's birth

lay, and he had ever so many beautiful presents. In the afternoon some little boys came to tea. They played games and talked and were very happy. Peter made me do all my tricks to show them, and they liked them so much that I had to do every one twice. I had plenty of lovely sweets given to me by the boys, and I wished Peter had a birthday every day. There were so many nice things to eat. Peter had a lovely

birthday cake with pink and
white icing on the top.

I thought it very strange
to have candles on a cake
I thought a few lovely bones
would have been just as
good as lighted candles.

The day after the party
I was in the garden when
a big rat came in. I had
never seen a rat before
though I had heard of them
when I was at the farm.
knew that all good terriers
chase them. So of course
I ran after it, and caught it

t was a very fierce rat,
nd bit my nose terribly.

But I did not seem to feel
much. I held on and
vould not let go until it
vas dead.

Everybody in the house
seemed to be very pleased
to think I had caught such
a big rat. They all said I
was a brave little dog. I
am afraid I was a little bit
stuck up over it too.

One or two days after I
had caught the rat, I was
alone in the kitchen when I
saw a pair of black boots
in the corner. Then I had
a splendid game with one
of them. I pretended it
was a rat. I shook it and
growled at it. And I threw

t about all over the room.
Then I started to play with
he other boot as well. It
was even more fun with
two, and I had a lovely
time chasing them all
round the kitchen. I slid
about all over the floor and
knocked a few things down.

I got so hot playing this
fine game that I really had
to sit down and rest a little.
While I was doing this, the
door opened and Cook came
in. I wagged my tail as
usual, but oh dear!—she

gave one look at me and
at the floor, then she made
such a fuss. I began to
think I was not so clever as
I had thought, and I felt
worse than ever when
Peter's daddy came in.
was given a whipping and
was put to bed for the rest
of the day. I was so sad.
So was Peter. He did not
like me to be punished, but
he said I must never do
such a thing again. So
now I only worry real rats
and not make-believe ones

CHAPTER III

The Fire

At night Peter sleeps in a room just at the top of the stairs, and I sleep in a basket just outside his door.

I like to feel I am near Peter to take care of him. I like to feel that I can guard the house too. I often sleep with one eye open, and if I hear a noise I go to see what it is.

One night when everyone

was asleep and the house
was very quiet, I fell asleep

too.　Suddenly I woke up
and smelt a very strang
smell coming from down

tairs. I went to see what
t was.

The smell came from the
kitchen, and I pushed the
loor open and went inside.
Then I knew what the
trange smell was. It was
moke.

I looked at the fireplace
nd saw that some clothes
hanging there were on fire,
nd the rug was smoking
oo. The smoke got in my
yes and nose and made
ne choke. But I knew I
nust tell Peter about it, so

I ran upstairs and scratched
at the door.

He did not answer, but
his father called out: " Lie
down, Patch, and be quiet.'
So I ran to his door and
scratched and barked loudly
After a moment he came to
the door and I could see he
was cross. He thought I
was making a noise for
nothing.

Then he smelt the smoke
too, and said: " Where is it
Patch?" I ran downstairs to
the kitchen and he came too.

There was more smoke by that time and some big flames. It was very hot too. Peter's father called very loudly for James.

James slept right at the very top of the house and he came running quickly down. Then they got lots and lots of water and at last the fire was put out.

When it was all over, they came up to Peter's room and patted my head and called me " good dog ".

" Thanks to you, old

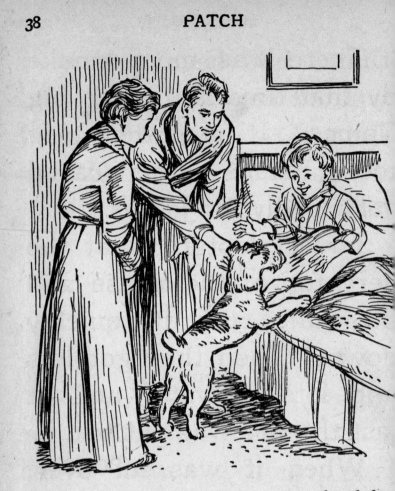

fellow," said Peter's daddy
" we are saved from having
the whole house burnt."

How glad I was to know

that I had been useful. I wanted to be good and clever like my mother and I wondered if she would ever hear about it.

CHAPTER IV

At the Seaside

One day Peter called me and I ran to him and jumped on his bed. It was in the morning, and the doctor who sometimes came to see him had just gone.

"Patch," cried Peter, hugging me, "what do you think? The doctor says I can begin to walk again, and we are going to the seaside."

I did not know what the seaside was, but I guessed it must be something very lovely as Peter was so excited. He was getting better quickly now, and every day he walked about a little.

One night, just at bed-time, Peter said: "Patch, we are going to-morrow.

Daddy is going to drive us in the car."

It was quite true, for the next day Mr. and Mrs. Ross and Peter got in the car with some luggage, and away we all went. We went for miles and miles and at last Peter cried:

"I can see the sea, Mummy. Oh look! Isn't it lovely?"

In a short while we had stopped at a little cottage, quite close to the sea, and somebody called Mrs. Brown

opened the door to us. W
all went in and had som
tea, and directly after wer
down to the sea.

I thought the sea wa
wonderful. Never befor
had I seen so much wat
all at once. I thought tl
duck pond at the farm wa
a very big one, but the se
was so very much bigge
and had waves on it to
The duck pond had 1
waves. There was ni
sand for me to run on, ar
wet sand for Peter to d

n as well as dry sand.
There were big rocks and

ittle pools, and many other
things as well.

We stayed by the sea for

many weeks. Peter go
stronger every day, and a
last he could run over the
sands with me. Sometime
he caught shrimps and
prawns in a net, and Mrs
Brown cooked them for his
tea.

One morning Peter said
to me: " Patch, I am going
to walk along the shore to
that little bay. I want to
hunt for shells."

Directly after breakfas
we set off, and soon reached
the bay.

Peter hunted about and picked up some very nice shells, quite different from those he had already found.

There was plenty of sand and we ran out to climb on some very high rocks.

Between the rocks were pools, some of them quite deep, with queer little creatures called crabs in them. Peter liked crabs very much. We stayed on the rocks for a long time. Peter's pa was quite full of shells, weed, and crabs.

Suddenly he cried: "Patch!
look at the sea. It is all

round us. Whatever shall
we do?"

It was true, the sea was
coming in to the shore again
ust as it did every day.

Peter had been so busy that he had forgotten about the tide, and there was a big piece of water between us and the shore.

It looked very deep, too deep for Peter to wade back, and the waves were coming over some of the rocks where we were standing.

I knew that I must get help very soon or Peter would be drowned, because he could not swim, although I could.

There was nobody in th
bay, so I knew it was of n
use to bark. I must d
something quickly. So
jumped up to Peter an
licked his face—to tell hin
not to worry. Then
jumped into the water and
swam towards the shore
It seemed a long way, and
the waves came over my
head several times.

Just as I was beginning
to feel very tired, a big
wave rolled me on to the
shore.

I looked round at Peter. He saw me and waved his cap.

As there was nobody on the beach I ran up a little path to the top of the cliff. There was a cottage not far off, something like the one where Mrs. Brown lived. I scratched at the door and barked loudly. A man opened it and said: "Here's a strange dog. Run away, this is not your home —go on, be off." I did not go away. I barked again very loudly, then ran back towards the path, and waited.

But he did not seem to understand that I wanted him to follow me.

Just then a boy came out and looked at me.

" It is the dog who is staying at Mrs. Brown's," he said. " It belongs to the little boy who has been ill."

I was so glad to hear him say that. I ran to him and tugged his coat, trying to pull him along. I wagged

my tail too—to show him I
was a friend.

"Look!" said the boy, "I

believe he wants us to go
with him. Let us follow
and see what it is. Good

dog," he said to me. "Show me the way."

Quickly I ran along to the top of the cliff and down the little path. They both ran with me.

I could see Peter was still on the rocks, but the sea had almost covered them.

"Get the boat, Dad," cried the boy. "There is some one on those big rocks, cut off by the tide."

Close to the cliff there was a hut, and the man

unlocked the door quickly. There was a boat inside, and they pushed it out. Directly I saw them do that, I knew they were going to save Peter, and I jumped into the boat too.

It was a motor boat and went very fast. We soon reached the rock where Peter stood. The sea had covered his feet, so we were only just in time.

How thankful I was when the man helped him into the boat! I jumped up to

Peter, wagged my tail, and
licked him for joy. Later
on that day, when Peter
was safe at home, every
body hugged and patted me
They said I had saved
Peter's life, and Peter said
I was the cleverest and
best dog in the world.

Peter's mother said we
must not go to the bay
again, so we did not, but
we had plenty of fun on
the sands and rocks near
Mrs. Brown's cottage.

CHAPTER V

Patch Catches a Burglar

At last the good times came to an end and we said good-bye to Mrs. Brown and the seaside.

Peter was sorry to leave the sea and the rocks and sand castles, but when we got home again it did really seem very nice.

I went straight to the garden where I had hidden some bones. I dug them up and they tasted delicious.

Then I felt quite happy again.

Peter went to school every day now. How I did miss him when he went! I sed to sit at the gate and ait for him to come home. Vhen I saw him coming own the road, I ran my astest to meet him, and I now he was just as glad ɔ see me as I was to see im, for he often told me so.

I had so many adventures vith Peter, that I haven't ime to tell you all of them. Iowever, I will tell you of ɔne which happened the irst winter I was there.

It was after Christmas, nd there had been plenty

of snow. Peter and I ha
been having splendid game
in the garden. Mr. Ros
had played snowballs wit
Peter, and they had mad
a fine snowman. I had
lovely time running afte
the snowballs, and bitin
them. So you can gues
how sorry we were whe
the rain came and spoi
it all.

By and by all the nic
clean white snow had gon

Then one day we ha
rain the whole day and

could only go out for a very short walk.

That night I was sleeping in my bed outside Peter's room when I woke up with a start. I listened for a moment and thought I heard a strange noise. The wind was blowing and making a noise too, so I thought I had made a mistake. I was just going to turn round and go to sleep again when I heard another noise.

Very quietly I got up and

went downstairs to see wha
it was. The noise seemed
to come from the dining
room, so I went there.

To my great surprise the
window was open and a
strange man was inside the
room.

I knew he was doing
wrong, so I barked as loudly
as I could and caught his
coat in my teeth.

He kicked me and I le
go for a moment. I barked
again and caught him once
more. He hit me severa

imes but I would not leave
go. I suddenly felt a dread-
ul pain in my head and I
ust fell down and did not
know any more.

When I opened my eyes
was on Peter's lap. He
was crying. I licked his
ace and he said:

" Patch—dear old Patch,
thought you were dead."

I wagged my tail, though
still felt very sick, and my
head   ached.   Then   Mr.
Ross and James came in.
They were talking.

I heard afterwards that
my barking had wakened
them, and then they had
heard the noise. They had
come downstairs and had
seen the thief give me that
dreadful bang on the head.
He had jumped out of the
window and they had chased
him. Then a policeman
helped them and at last
the thief was caught and
taken away.

Everybody was so kind
to me. Peter and his
mother hugged me many

mes, and even Cook said
was a fine brave dog.
Ir. Ross said:

" Patch—old man. You
re the best dog in the
vorld and worth your
veight in gold."

I certainly was the proud-
st dog in the world, and
vhen Peter put on me a
ovely silver collar, I was
he happiest as well as the
roudest dog.

I am quite grown up now,
nd Peter is a big boy. We
;o out for long walks very

often in the country lan
and through green fields.

I love Peter very dearl
and I know he loves me
and as he is the best maste
in the world—why, I am th
luckiest dog!